Henry Charles Lea

Translations

and other Rhymes

Henry Charles Lea

Translations
and other Rhymes

ISBN/EAN: 9783337270414

Printed in Europe, USA, Canada, Australia, Japan

Cover: Foto ©Andreas Hilbeck / pixelio.de

More available books at **www.hansebooks.com**

AND

OTHER RHYMES.

BY

HENRY C. LEA.

(PRIVATELY PRINTED.)

PHILADELPHIA:

1882.

CONTENTS.

(iii)

A CRUSADER'S FAREWELL.

(THIBAULT DE CHAMPAGNE.)

[Presumably written in 1238, when Thibault was about to set out at the
head of the French Crusaders. The cruel lady of his love was the
Queen Regent, Blanche of Navarre, mother of St. Louis.]

DEAR lady! thus it is that I must go,
    Leaving the pleasant land where I have borne
  And suffered all the ills that man may know:
    Yet, leaving thee, I hold myself in scorn.
God! why exists yon land of paynim foe,
Which works so many faithful lovers' woe?
  Lovers whose severed hearts in absence yearn,
Till they forget that love can joy bestow.

Dear lady! without love I cannot be,
    For to it all my thoughts and hopes aspire,
And my true heart will never set me free,
    But blindly follows where may lead desire.

Yet hath love's lesson been so hard to me,
That how to linger here I scarce can see,
  Denied all hope of her whom all admire—
The loveliest dame that e'er heard lover's plea.

Away from thee, I ask myself in vain
  What joy earth yet can have for me in store;
For never aught has given me such pain
  As leaving thee.   My heavy heart is sore
To think that never we may meet again.
Full oft shall I seek vainly to restrain
  Bitter repentance as I leave this shore,
And thy dear voice seems murmuring through my brain.

O sweet Lord God ! behold, to Thee I fly,
  Leaving for Thee what I have held so dear;
Well may I hope from Thee some guerdon high,
  Since for Thy sake I lose all earthly cheer.
Now for Thy service all prepared am I.
Sweet Christ! to Thee I give most trustfully
  Myself; no better lord can I revere;
For who serves Thee upon Thee can rely.

My heart is filled with grief and joyfulness—
  Grieving that from my lady love I part,
Joyful, because at last do I profess
  To serve the Lord, who is both soul and heart.

This is the love which words may not express,
Which wisest men seek ever to possess—
　The pearl, the ruby, that relieves the smart
Of the foul sins through which weak men transgress.

And Thou, Heaven's Queen, who hast such power to bless,
Our Lady! succor me in sore distress.
　Let me love Thee: my lady's loss convert
To gain, becoming Thou my patroness!

A CRUSADER'S LAMENT.

(THE COMTE DE POITIERS.)

[Written on his departure for the First Crusade by Guillaume IX. Duc
d'Aquitaine and Comte de Poitou (1088 to 1126), who was re-
nowned both for his poetry and his gallantries. The Fulk of Anjou
alluded to is Foulques Rechin, one of the most troublesome barons of
the day.]

I GO, alas! to exile far
　Leaving my son in strife and war,
　In dread of many a battle scar,
　　From all the lords and barons near.

Since thus I'm forced to bid adieu
To my broad lordship of Poitou,
I leave brave Fulco of Anjou
    To guard it and his kinsman dear.

If Fulco will not succor bring,
As well as our liege lord the king,
Seeing his youth, they'll surely wring
    From him his lands and castles here.

I leave what dearest is to me,
The pomp and pride of chivalry,
To wander far beyond the sea,
    Where sinners find the fate they fear.

THE CHURCH.

(FROM " LA GESTA DE FRA PEYRE CARDINAL.")

[Pierre Cardinal was a troubadour of noble birth and high consideration
at the courts of Toulouse and Aragon. His life is said to have ex-
tended from 1206 to 1306. He was no heretic, and his arraignment
of the church reflects the views then prevalent throughout southern
Europe as to the ecclesiastical abuses of the time.]

I SEE the Pope his sacred trust betray,
For, while the rich his grace can gain alway,
   His favors from the poor are aye withholden.
He strives to gather wealth as best he may,
Forcing Christ's people blindly to obey,
   So that he may repose in garments golden.
The vilest traffickers in souls are all
His chapmen, and for gold a prebend's stall
   He'll sell them, or an abbacy or mitre,
And to us he sends clowns and tramps who crawl,
Vending his pardon-letters, from cot to hall—
   Letters and pardons worthy of the writer,
   Which leave our pokes, if not our sins, the lighter.

No better is each honored cardinal.
From early morning's dawn to evening's fall

Their time is passed in eagerly contriving
To drive some bargain foul with each and all.
So if you feel a want, or great or small,
    Or if for some preferment you are striving,
The more you please to give the more 'twill bring,
Be it a purple cap or bishop's ring.
    And it need ne'er in any way alarm you
That you are ignorant of everything
To which a minister of Christ should cling—
    You will have revenue enough to warm you;
    And bear in mind that lesser gifts won't harm you.

Our bishops, too, are plunged in similar sin,
For pitilessly they flay the very skin
    From all their priests who chance to have fat livings.
For gold their seal official you can win
To any writ, no matter what's therein.
    Sure God alone can make them stop their thievings.
'Twere hard, in full, their evil works to tell,
As when, for a few pence, they greedily sell
    The tonsure to some mountebank or jester,
Whereby the temporal courts are wronged as well,
For thus these tonsured rogues they cannot quell,
    Howe'er their scampish doings us may pester,
    While round the church still growing evils fester.

Then as for all the priests and minor clerks,
Too many of them, God knows, there are whose works
   And daily life belie their daily preaching.
Scarce better are they than so many Turks,
Though they, no doubt, may be well taught—it irks
   Not me to own the fulness of their teaching,
For, learned or ignorant, they are content
To make a traffic of each sacrament,
   The Mass's holy sacrifice included.
And when they shrive an honest penitent,
Who will not bribe, his penance they augment,
   For honesty should never be obtruded—
   All which, by sinners fair, is easily eluded.

'Tis true the monks and friars make ample show
Of rigors which by rule they undergo,
   But this the vainest is of all pretences,
In sooth, they live full twice as well, we know,
As e'er they did at home, despite their vow,
   And all their mock parade of abstinences.
No jollier life than theirs can be, indeed ;
And specially the begging friars exceed,
   Whose frock grants license as abroad they wander.
These motives 'tis which to the Orders lead
So many worthless men, in sorest need
   Of pelf which on their vices they may squander,
   And then, the frock protects them in their plunder.

BALLADE.

(CHARLES DUC D'ORLÉANS.)

On the death of his wife, written in his English prison, after
Agincourt, 1415.

A H Death ! what hath emboldened thee
    To snatch that fair and noble dame—
  She who was everything to me,
    Of all my thoughts the single aim ?
    Since thus my mistress thou dost claim,
Why hast thou not me also ta'en !
  For I with thee would rather go
  Than linger here in cureless wo,
In torment, misery, and pain !

Ah ! she was bright and fair to see,
  Radiant with youth's most joyous flame.
I pray God that thou cursed be,
  False Death, who could such beauty maim.
  Hadst thou but stayed till old age came,
I 'd not so bitterly arraign
  That felon deed, that hasty blow,
  Which leaves me mourning here below,
In torment, misery, and pain.

Ah ! lonely left, thus torn from thee,
　Sweet lady, joy is but a name,
Since love must yield to Death's decree !
　Yet hear my promise, that the same
　Heart-service thou mayst still reclaim
From me, in earnest prayers to gain
　Thy soul's release ; while here I know
　But sharp regrets, as years shall flow
In torment, misery, and pain.

O God ! who o'er all things dost reign,
In thy sweet grace and mercy, deign
　On her forgiveness to bestow,
　So that not long her soul may grow
In torment, misery, and pain !

BALLADE.

(VILLON.)

IN what far land, pray, tell me true,
　Is Flora, Rome's most noted fair ?
Where is Archippa, Thaïs too —
　In beauty a right royal pair ?
　And Echo, who replies, where'er
O'er lake or stream your voice may go—

Whose beauty mortal may not share?
But where, too, is last winter's snow?

Where is wise Heloïse, who drew
    Unwitting, to the cruel snare,
Poor Abelard, and made him rue
    His love in monkhood's endless care?
    Where, also, is that queen so rare
Who learned Buridan did throw,
    Ensacked in Seine's swift current there?
But where, too, is last winter's snow?

That Queen, Blanche, both in name and hue,
    Whose song with Siren's might compare?
Beatrice, Bertha, Alice, too,
    And Eremberge, of Maine the heir?
    And Joan of Arc, whom, in despair,
At Rouen burned the English foe.
    Where are they, Blessed Virgin, where?
But where, too, is last winter's snow?

ENVOI.

Prince, vain enquiry wisely spare,
    Nor seek where these may be to know,
Lest you but hear this refrain bare—
    But where, too, is last winter's snow?

CHANSON.

Written by FRANCIS I. while captive in Spain.

WHEN we rejoice amid adversity,
Why then adversity's foul self we see,
Even in its triumph o'er prosperity,
Is overcome.

We also see that absolute truth in some
Firm steadfast bosom never need succumb
To falsehood, which grows ever faint and dumb
As time rolls on.

And therefore do I count myself as one
Contented, though my hopes be overthrown,
For well I wot the good that comes alone
From my own mind,

Which is not by these prison bars confined,
But wanders freely as the joyous wind,
Through endless maze of thoughts all intertwined
And ever new.

For naught a man's free spirit can subdue,
Nor bind his resolute will to laws untrue;
But it is purified and strengthened through
The travail sore.

Which serves to comfort him who bears it, for
All trial but emboldens him the more,
And the stout heart on honor sets its store
    And naught beside.

The heart rests victor, though the hand be tied ;
In toil alone will happiness abide;
Firm will against ill-fortune sets its pride
    And deems it naught.

Whence I conclude that well that deed was wrought
Through which I 've learned that fortune 's but a thought,
When steadfastness has once its lesson taught.
    And what think ye?

RONDEAU.

(CLÉMENT MAROT.)

IN the old time, love needed not this train
    Of splendid gifts and idle flattering show.
    A lover then would rate the world below
    The simplest toy his mistress might bestow,
For heart outspoke to heart in language plain.
    And if 'twere crowned with bliss, say, do ye know
    How love would last? Why, thirty years or so ;

Through life unchanged affection would remain,
In the old time.

But now we scorn what we to true love owe.
Falsehood and fickleness unblushing reign.
Then, damsels, if ye would my heart enchain,
First bring back love as it was long ago,
As fond, as true as it was wont to glow
In the old time!

DIFFIDENCE.

(IMITATED FROM RONSARD.)

WHEN from the laughing group apart,
I saw thee wandering, sad and slow,
Communing with thy secret heart,
And listening its sweet accents low,
I longed, O how I longed! to speak,
To breathe my earnest prayer to thee,
Again to call unto thy cheek
The tender smile I love to see!

But ah! my fluttering heart denied
My voice; true love is timid ever.
In vain to meet thy glance I tried,
Confused I shrank from the endeavor.

If thou canst read my looks aright,
Or heed the sighs I fain would quell,
Then wilt thou learn, in my despite,
The tale my tongue can never tell !

THE POET'S GRAVE.

(RONSARD.)

YE sombre caves, ye fountains,
That from yon rugged mountains,
Leap sparkling forth, and glide
With laughing tide ;

Ye mystic woodland shades,
Ye dim and leafy glades,
Ye winding rivers, hear
My earnest prayer.

When heaven and fate decree
My death, and I shall see
No more the awakening ray
Of each new day;

I crave no lofty tomb,
In old cathedral gloom,
To mock, but ne'er delay
My sure decay.

No, make for me a grave
Where trees their branches wave,
Tossing their green arms wide
    In joyous pride.

From me, let ivy springing,
In endless verdure, clinging
O'er every rock and flower
    My grave embower.

There let the wild vine spread
Its tendrils o'er my head,
Guarding with shadows deep
    My quiet sleep!

THE JESUITS.

(DE BÉRANGER.)

[Though not in themselves remarkable, these verses fairly illustrate the unceasing warfare which, for nearly a generation, de Béranger waged against all abuses of authority, temporal and spiritual, gaining thereby a popularity, inherited by Victor Hugo, which is one of the moral as well as political phenomena of the century.]

TO Saint Ignatius, patron sought
    By our small saints of modern times,
    Give honor for the wonder wrought
    Which I relate in these few rhymes.

By treachery which would be most
Shameful, if Saints could be misled,
He made the Devil give up the ghost—
The Devil is dead, the Devil is dead!

For Satan, finding him at table,
Cried "Drink with me, or shame be thine!"
The saint, with craft most censurable,
Mixed holy water in the wine.
Poor Satan drinks, and taken sick
With colic, writhes in pain and dread,
Then dies, like any heretic—
The Devil is dead, the Devil is dead!

"Alas, he's dead!" the monks all cry,
"Who'll purchase now our blessed wares?"
"And who," the priests respond, "will buy
Henceforth our Masses and our prayers?"
The Papal conclave, in despair,
See power and wealth forever fled—
"We've lost our father," they declare,
"The Devil is dead, the Devil is dead!

"For we shall seek, through love, in vain
The liberal gifts which fear inspires;
And who will rouse for us again
Fell persecution's waning fires?

If man to escape our yoke can hope
    The light of Truth abroad will spread,
God will be greater than the Pope—
    The Devil is dead, the Devil is dead!"

Ignatius answers, "Give me then
    The Devil's office and his power.
He long since ceased to frighten men,
    While I will make even monarchs cower.
Plagues, wars, and massacres, and thievings
    Will bring such wealth you 'll all be fed,
Till God shall only have our leavings—
    The Devil is dead, the Devil is dead!"

"On thy shrewd head may blessings come,
    And on thy venomed wit!" they cry.
His Order soon, the prop of Rome,
    Sees its black robe affright the sky.
"Now," say the pitying angels, "well
    May tears for man's sad lot be shed.
Ignatius is the heir of Hell—
    The Devil is dead, the Devil is dead?"

DESPAIR.

(HENRI MURGER.)

"WHO knocks so loudly at the door?"
  "Open, 'tis I!" "Thy name, I pray.
At midnight, though my home be poor,
  None enters in such heedless way."

"Open!" "Thy name?" "The snow falls fast,
  Open!" "Thy name?" "Quick, let me come!"
"What is thy name?" "In this chill blast,
  No corpse were colder in the tomb.

"I've wandered far, from east to west,
  From south to north, in cold and wet;
Benumbed and worn, now let me rest
  A space beside thy fire!" "Not yet!

"What is thy name?" "They call me Glory,
  Deathless is he with whom I stay."
"Begone! thou phantom nugatory!"
  "I pray thee drive me not away,

"For I am Love, and Joy, and Youth,
  Heaven's choicest blessings, half divine!"
"Begone! She whom I loved, in sooth,
  Long since hath left me here to pine."

" But I am Art and Poesy,
   Proscribed by all ; quick, open !''   "Go !
No more I sing my faithless she,
   Her very name no more I know.''

"Open to me, for Wealth am I ;
   I bring thee gold in ample store.
Thy mistress I can for thee buy.''
   "But canst thou make us love once more?''

"Open to me, for I am Power :
   Earth's thrones are mine !''   " Delusions all !
Canst thou bring back the vanished hour ?
   Canst thou the much-loved dead recall?''

"Since thou wilt not thy door unbar
   Unless the guest his name disclose,
Know I am Death, who bring from far
   The only cure for human woes !''

" Enter, grim stranger, enter here,
   Disdain not this abode unblessed.
'Tis poverty, forlorn and drear,
   That hails thee as a welcome guest.

"Enter.   Long have I weary been
   Of life without a hope or tie.

Oft have I longed thy sleep to win,
  But lacked the fortitude to die.

"I 've waited for thee, nor in vain.
  Lead on, I 'll gladly follow thee.
But spare my dog, for I would fain
  Some creature here should grieve for me!"

THE MINSTREL.

(GOETHE.)

"WHAT is 't I hear before the gate?
      What sounds so sweet are ringing?
    'Twere fitting in our hall of state
      To listen to such singing!"
As the king spoke, the pages flew
And quick returned. The king anew
  Cried "Bring the old man hither!"

"Hail to you all, my noble lords,
  Hail to you, lovely ladies!
What a rich heaven! Who could, in words,
  Tell each star that here arrayed is?
Be closed mine eyes! In such a maze
Of splendor there 's no time to gaze
  On all that here displayed is!"

He closed his eyes, and at the word
    Burst forth in strains so thrilling,
The knights with martial fire were stirred,
    While tears fair eyes were filling.
Pleased with the song and singer bold,
The king bade fetch a chain of gold
    To honor him for his singing.

" Give not the golden chain to me,
    But to your knights, whose glances
Of fiery valor love to see
    The foemen's splintered lances.
Or give it to your chancellor
And let him add one burden more
    To those he already carries.

"I sing as sing the birds who dwell
    In springtime 'mid the bushes.
The song rewards the singer well
    When from the heart it gushes.
But might one guerdon more be mine,
I 'd crave a draught of generous wine,
    In golden mazer blushing."

He took the bowl and drained it all—
    " O draught of sweetest savor !
How blest the house must be where small
    Is reckoned such a favor !

If all goes well, think well of me,
And thank the Lord as fervently
As for this draught I thank you!"

THE LOVED-ONE EVER NEAR.

(GOETHE.)

I THINK of thee when the sun's dawning splendor
    Breaks o'er the sea.
When on the fountains play the moonbeams tender,
    I think of thee!

I see thee when, upon the road-side weary,
    The dust-clouds rise,
And when the wanderer threads his pathway dreary,
    Neath starless skies!

I hear thee where the sounding billows riot,
    In angriest moods:
I go to listen in the perfect quiet
    Of slumbering woods!

I am with thee! Though distant thou, this even,
    Still art thou near!
The stars shed their sweet light on me from heaven—
    O wert thou here!

THE ERL-KING.

(GOETHE.)

WHO rides thus late through the night so wild?
'Tis the father bearing his little child.
With tender care, in his sheltering arm,
He holds him safely, he keeps him warm.

"My son, why hid'st thou thy face with fear?"
"Seest thou not, father, the Erl-King near?
The Erl-King near, with his crown and train?"
"My son, it is but the mist and rain."

"Come, dear child, come hither with me.
The prettiest games will I play with thee.
The loveliest flowers are blooming there,
And golden robes shalt thou have to wear!"

"O father, father, dost thou not hear
The Erl-King's promise in whispers clear?"
"Be quiet, keep quiet, my little child,
'Tis the rustling leaves in the forest wild."

"Dear child, sweet child, wilt thou go with me?
My daughters shall watch thee tenderly.
My daughters, who through the night-dance sweep,
Shall rock thee, and dance thee, and sing thee to sleep!"

"O father, father, and seest thou not
The Erl-King's daughters in yon dark spot?"
" My son, my son, there is nothing here
Save the willows old that so gray appear."

" I love thee, child, for thy beauty.   Nay,
An thou wilt not come, I must force thee away!"
" O father, father! I feel his clutch,
The Erl-King hurts me, he hurts me much!"

The father shuddered : his steed he pressed,
While the moaning child he clasped to his breast.
Through the toilsome way to his home he sped—
In his loving arms his child lay dead.

TO MY MOTHER.

(HEINE.)

I LEFT thee once, my spirit madly burning,
To wander onwards to earth's farthest shore,
And find if I could quench the thirst 1 bore
For love and satisfy my heart's wild yearning.

So love I sought, through every pathway turning :
With outstretched hand I went from door to door,
Begging a little love from each one's store,
But they gave only cruel hate and spurning.

And thus in quest of love I wandered ever,
Seeking for love, and finding love, ah never!
Then homeward turned, spent with the vain endeavor.

And thou didst come with hasty step to meet me,
And what in thine o'erbrimming eyes did greet me—
That was the love whose quest so long did cheat me!

TO ———.

(HEINE.)

THE yellow foliage trembles
    And the leaves fall to their doom.
  Ah! all that is dear and lovely
    Shrivels and seeks the tomb.

A saddened sunshine glimmers
    Round the tops of the fading grove,
Like the farewell kiss of summer,
    Departing with life and love.

And the tears spring forth unbidden
    From the depths of my aching heart,
As the scene recalls too nearly
    The hour that saw us part.

When I was forced to leave thee,
Though I knew that death was nigh,
And I was the parting summer,
And thou wast the leaves that die.

THE PILGRIMAGE TO REVLAAR.

(HEINE.)

I.

THE mother stood at the window,
The youth lay on his bed.
"Come look at the procession,
Come, Wilhelm dear," she said.

"I am so sick, O mother,
I can neither hear nor see.
I think of the dead Gretchen,
And my heart aches wofully."

"Rise, and we'll go to Revlaar,
With book and rosary.
God's Mother there will surely
Cure thy sick heart for thee."

Now swells the chanting solemn,
   The Church's banners shine,
As on goes the procession,
   Through Cöllen on the Rhine.

As the crowd sweeps on, the mother
   Leads her son tenderly,
And both join in the chorus—
   "Sweet Mary, praise to Thee !"

II.

The Mother of God at Revlaar
   Wears to-day her richest gear.
She has much to do, for gather
   Sick folk from far and near.

And these poor sick ones bring her,
   As offerings to suit,
Limbs made of wax so neatly—
   Full many a hand and foot.

And whoso a wax hand offers,
   She frees his hand of pain ;
And whoso a wax foot offers,
   His foot is made whole again

And many who went on crutches
  On the rope can dance a round ;
And many can play on the viol
  Who had not a finger sound.

The mother has taken a candle
  And a waxen heart has made—
"Take this to God's sweet Mother,
  She will heal thy grief," she said.

The son takes the wax heart, sighing,
  To the shrine he sighing goes ;
The tears from his eyes are flowing,
  As the prayer from his sick heart flows.

"Thou Blessed of all the Blessed,
  Thou Queen upon Heaven's throne,
Thou God's own purest Virgin,
  To Thee be my sorrows known !

" I dwell alone with my mother,
  At Cöllen on the Rhine,
Cöllen where there is many
  A church and chapel and shrine.

"And near to us dwelt Gretchen,
  Who now lies 'neath the ground—
Mary, I bring Thee a wax heart,
  Heal thou my heart's deep wound !

" Heal thou my heart that 's broken,
  And I will most fervently
Sing every night and morning,
  Sweet Mary, praise to Thee !"

III.

The sick son and his mother
  In a room together slept.
The Mother of God came thither,
  And silently in she stepped.

The sick youth she bent over,
  And on his heart so seared
She laid her hand, and softly
  She smiled and disappeared.

In her sleep all this the mother
  Saw—and yet more she marked.
From her slumber she awakened,
  For the dogs so loudly barked.

There lay, stretched out before her,
Her son, all stark and dead,
While o'er his wan, shrunk features,
The dawn its radiance shed.

Her hands she gently folded—
Benumbed with grief was she,
Yet her low voice rose devoutly—
"Sweet Mary, praise to Thee !"

LORELEI.

(HEINE.)

I CANNOT tell what means it
That I so sad should be.
'Tis but an old-time story
That haunts my memory.

Cool is the air in the twilight,
As the Rhine steals on its way;
O'er the crest of the distant mountain,
Glimmers the parting day.

And aloft there sits a maiden,
  A maiden wondrous fair;
Glistens her golden kirtle,
  As she combs her golden hair.

With a golden comb she combs it,
  While in witching tone she sings,
A lay in whose sweet cadence
  A strange weird music rings.

With wild desire it masters
  The youth in his little skiff;
His eyes are fixed on the maiden,
  He heeds not the hidden reef.

I believe that the end of the story
  Is the sinking of skiff and youth,
And that mischief with her singing
  Hath the Lorelei wrought in sooth!

THE MINSTREL'S CURSE.

(UHLAND.)

A PALACE vast and lofty there stood in days of yore,
With towers that proudly glistened, far to the distant
shore;
Around it fragrant gardens lay rich with endless
flowers,
And fountains whose bright waters wove fairy rain-
bow showers.

There dwells a haughty monarch, whom no foes dare assail,
There on his throne he sitteth, so dark and yet so pale:
And what he thinks is terror, and what he looks is scath,
And what he speaks is torture, and what he writes is death.

Now hither come two minstrels, in sooth a noble pair,
The one with golden ringlets, the other with snowy hair:
Bearing his harp, the elder a gallant palfrey rides,
With lightsome step beside him his blooming comrade strides.

"Prepare thyself, my son," thus the elder minstrel says,
"With fullest voice to render our deepest, loftiest lays.
Gather all strength that may from all human passions spring,
Our song to-day must soften the fierce heart of the king!"

Now stand the noble minstrels in a hall of royal sheen,
Upon the throne are sitting the king and his fair queen—
He fearful in his splendor as the blood red Northern light,
She soft and mild and tender as a moonbeam through the
  night.

Then the old man sweeps the harp-strings with a skill that
  hath no peer,
So that richer, ever richer, the sound swells on the ear :
While at every pause the youth's voice uprises clear and free,
As it were a spirit choir in heavenly melody.

They sing of love and springtime, of the ancient golden days,
Of freedom and of manhood, and of God's mysterious ways,
Of all the earthly longings by which the heart is riven,
Of all the holy raptures which uplift the soul to heaven.

The circling crowd of courtiers their mockeries forbear,
The king's most grizzled warriors bow humbly down in
  prayer,
The queen, with heart 'twixt sadness and struggling joy op-
  pressed,
Hath thrown unto the minstrels the rose that decked her
  breast.

"Ye have seduced my people, my wife would ye mislead?"
Thus shrieks the king, all trembling with wrath from foot to
  head.

His sword, like bolt of lightning, at the youth's breast he
    throws,
Whence in place of golden music, the richest life-blood flows.

Like storm-tossed leaves the courtiers scatter in wild alarm,
While the youth gasps out his spirit on his aged master's arm,
Who wraps him in his mantle and sets him on his horse,
And, with his weary burden, from the castle takes his course.

Yet before the lofty entrance he tarries for a space,
And upon a marble column, which arose in lofty grace,
His much loved harp he shivers, of all harps the most rare,
As his voice through hall and gardens rings like a trumpet
    blare.

"Woe to thee, thou proud castle!   No gladsome song or
    word,
Through all thy pillared chambers, shall e'er again be heard !
No ! naught but sighs and groaning, and the craven step of
    slaves,
Till his torch o'er thy dark ruin the avenging spirit waves !

"Woe to ye, fragrant gardens, that smile in May's sweet
    light !
Look on these disfigured features of him that was as bright,
That looking ye may wither, your fountains all be dry,
And ye may in future ages a stony desert lie !

"And woe to thee, fell murderer! Thou curse of min
    strelsy!
All vain thy frantic strivings for bloody honors be!
Let thy name in darkness buried be blind Oblivion's share,
As the groan of one that dieth is lost in empty air!"

High heaven has heard and answered the aged minstrel's cry.
Those stately walls have fallen, those halls in ruins lie.
Yet to show their ancient splendor, one sculptured pillar tall
Stands, riven through the centre, and tottering to its fall.

And in place of fragrant gardens, a waste of desert land,
Where no tree invites with shelter, and no spring can pierce
    the sand.
That monarch's name no sagas, his deeds no lays rehearse—
All buried and forgotten! Such is the minstrel's curse!

THE CASTLE BY THE SEA.

(UHLAND.)

HAST seen the lofty castle,
    The castle by the sea?
Golden and rosy o'er it,
    The smiling cloudlets be.

The cliff it might bend over
 To the clear flood below,
Or seek the clouds that hover
 In evening's tender glow.

"Well have I marked the castle,
 The castle by the sea,
With the pale moonbeams o'er it,
 While mists around it flee."

The wind and wave's wild music,
 Joyous was it and free?
Echoed those halls so lofty
 With song and revelry?

" In deep and solemn silence
 Were winds and wavelets all,
Heard I a dirge of sorrow,
 With weeping, from the hall."

Sawest thou upon the terrace
 Walk forth the king and queen,
The wave of the crimson mantle,
 The coronet's golden sheen?

And led they not with rapture,
  A blooming maiden there,
As gladsome as a sunbeam,
  With glittering, golden hair?

"Well did I mark the parents,
  No crown had they, I wot,
But clad in sable garments—
  The maiden saw I not!"

HONOR TO WOMAN.

(SCHILLER.)

HONOR to woman! On life's earthly river
Heavenly roses she flingeth for ever,
  Love's blessed chaplet with rapture she forms.
Modestly shrinking, her loveliness veiling,
Vestal-like feeds she the fire unfailing
  Which to each noble aim man's spirit warms.

Man's unruly strength forever
  Strays within the bounds of wrong.
Reckless wanders his endeavor
  Passion's wayward path along.

Always future hopes pursuing,
    Never is his heart at rest.
Each dream-image fiercely wooing,
    To the stars he 'd urge the quest.

Woman, entreating, bewitching, enchanting,
Homeward decoying her fugitive panting,
    Bids him to live in the life of the hour.
Daughter unspoiled of kind, motherly Nature,
Quietly seeking to bless every creature,
    Rests she forever in Nature's sweet bower.

        Man, with eager, thoughtless striving
            Ever seeks to force his way.
        Friend and foe before him driving,
            Asks not rest, nor brooks delay.
        Making now, and now unmaking,
            Sport of every fresh desire,
        Which, like Hydra-heads are taking
            New forms as the old expire.

Woman, untouched by these passions consuming,
Gathers the flowers that around her are blooming,
    Gathers and guards them from tempest and wrong,
Freer than man, in the limits she prizes,
Richer than he in the lore he despises,
    And in the infinite circle of song.

Man's heart, proud and self-sufficing,
   Knows not the divine delight
Hearts can feel in sacrificing
   Each to each, in love's sweet plight.
Soul which shares another's feeling
   Knows not he, whom tears ne'er blest.
Life's stern strife is ever steeling
   Harder still his hardened breast.

E'en as the wind-harp's sweet cadences waken,
Faint though the Zephyr by which it be shaken,
   So woman's kindliness ever appears.
Tenderly moved by all suffering and sorrow,
Swells the fair bosom, the loving eyes borrow
   Heaven's own pearls in compassionate tears.

   Man, in his dominion, only
      Knows the insolent law of might.
   Cultured Persia bendeth pronely
      'Neath the Scythian's sabre bright.
   Passions wild and ever wilder
      Furious with each other vie,
   And fell Eris rules, whence milder
      Charis hath been forced to fly.

Woman, with winning and gentle persuasion,
Guards her love-kingdom from every invasion,

Lulling all strife in the slumber of peace,
Luring the forces oppugnant together,
Binding them fast in her magical tether,
Teaching the discord primeval to cease !

THE ERL-KING'S DAUGHTER.

(HERDER.)

SIR Olaf was riding far and wide
To bid his friends to his wedding tide.

He met the elves in their woodland play,
And the Erl-King's daughter barred the way.

"Welcome, Sir Olaf! why wouldst thou flee?
Come take thy place in the dance with me!"

"I may not dance, I may not stay,
To-morrow it is my bridal day."

"Listen, Sir Olaf, come dance with me,
And two golden spurs will I give to thee,

"With a garment of silk so pure and white,
Which my mother bleached in the full moon's light!"

"I may not dance, I may not stay,
To-morrow it is my bridal day."

"Listen, Sir Olaf, come dance with me,
And a pile of gold will I give to thee."

"Thy pile of gold I would gladly share,
But to dance I neither will nor dare."

"An thou wilt not, Sir Olaf, dance with me,
Sickness and plague shall follow thee!"

With that she smote him upon the heart,
Never had felt he such deadly smart.

On his horse the pallid youth she threw —
"Now get thee back to thy maiden true!"

And when at last he reached his home,
His mother trembled to see him come.

"My son, my son, what doth thee ail,
That thy cheek should be so wan and pale?"

"Full well it may be pale and wan,
Since I to the Erl King's land have gone."

"My son, my son, my joy and pride,
What shall I say to thy coming bride?"

" Tell her I 've gone to the wood near by
My horse and hound for a space to try."

Next morn, before one could fairly see,
There came the bride and her company.

They drank of the mead and the wine so red—
" Where is Sir Olaf, my groom ?" she said.

" Sir Olaf has gone to the wood near by,
His horse and hound for a space to try."

The bride lifted up the mantle red—
There lay Sir Olaf, and he was dead !

THE FIGHT WITH THE DRAGON.

(SCHILLER.)

I.

THROUGH the long street why pours the crowd?
Rushing in haste with clamor loud ?
Is Rhodes laid waste with fire, that here
Like storm·clouds press her people near?
I mark, high o'er the surging mass,
A knight on mettled charger pass,

But what is that strange form I see
Dragged after him with frantic glee?
It seems a dragon in its shape,
  With cruel wide-distended jaw;
On it, by turns, the people gape,
  And on the knight, with growing awe.

II.

And now a thousand voices rise—
" Come, see the dragon, there it lies,
That slew our flocks and shepherds ! There,
Too, is the knight that slew the slayer !
Before him, many a gallant knight
Went forth to dare the unequal fight—
Went forth, but to return no more :
Then honors on the hero pour !"
Thus onward surged the crowd along,
  Straight to the cloister, where, in haste
Assembled, sate the knightly throng
  Whom St. John's pious Order graced.

III.

Before the noble Master's seat
The modest youth pays homage meet.
The crowds pour after him, until
The stairways ample bounds they fill.

The youth begins: " I have but done
The duty which no knight may shun.
The dragon which laid waste the land
Lies harmless, slaughtered by this hand.
The wayfarer no more need fear,
  The hind may lead his flocks in peace,
The pilgrim seek the pathway sheer
  Up to our Lady's House of Grace."

IV.

Sternly the Master bends his brow:
"A hero's deed is thine, I trow.
Valor is what becomes a knight,
And thine is proved in desperate fight.
But tell me the first duty laid
Upon the knight, with Cross arrayed,
And pledged to fight for Christ our Lord?"
Then pale with fear grew all who heard.
But he with noble calmness spake,
  Bending in low obeisance there,
" Obedience, first of all, doth make
  Us worthy of the Cross we bear."

V.

" This duty, then," the Prince replied,
" Thy headstrong will hath set aside.

The combat which the law forbade
With wanton heart hast thou essayed."
Calmly the youth replied : "Withhold
Thy judgment till my tale is told.
The law's design and true intent
Most fully to obey I meant.
Not recklessly went I to dare
    With that dread beast a combat vain :
I sought, through art and prudence rare,
    The hoped-for victory to gain.

VI.

" Five dauntless brethren of the Cross,
Our Order's pride, Religion's loss,
Fell, ere thou didst forbid each knight
Again to tempt the hopeless fight.
Yet still my heart was torn within
By fierce desires that fight to win.
The quiet nights brought no repose,
I from dream-combats panting rose,
Only with each new dawn to learn
    Of added suffering, further woe,
And ever wilder longings burn,
    Till I resolve to dare the foe.

VII.

"And with myself I argued then:
What chiefly honors youths and men?
What were the deeds of heroes bold,
Whose names were sung by bards of old,
Whom the blind Paynim raised on high
As gods to dwell beyond the sky?
'Twas that the groaning earth they freed
From monsters by each valorous deed.
That the poor victims might be spared,
   They grappled with Minotaur dread,
The Lion's rage in fight they dared,
   And lavishly their blood they shed.

VIII.

" Is it the Saracen abhorred
Alone who fits the Christian's sword?
Is misbelief his only foe?
He is sent to save the world from woe!
His strong arm should deliverance bring
From every care and suffering.
But wisdom should his courage guide
And strength with prudence be allied.
Thus oft I reasoned as I went,
   The monster's lair to view alone,

And when to me the thought was sent,
  Joyous I cried : The task is done !

IX.

" From thee permission craved I then
To seek my native land again.
Freely thou yieldedst to my prayer,
And prosperous gales soon brought me there.
Scarce did I reach the well-known strand
When, through an artist's cunning hand,
That dragon-shape I framed anew,
To every well-marked feature true.
Short were the legs which bore the mass,
  Upreared, of that huge body's weight ;
The back, all round, with scales of brass
  Was clothed, which naught might penetrate.

X.

" High rose the neck in lofty state,
And, ghastly as Hell's open gate,
As though to fill its ravenous maw,
Wide stretched its all-devouring jaw.
From the black gorge, above, beneath,
Shone grimly forth sharp rows of teeth ;

A sword's point seems the tongue, while flies
Sharp lightning from its beady eyes.
The monstrous length of back, drawn out,
   Becomes a snake, whose winding course,
In volumed folds is cast about,
   As though to envelop man and horse.

XI.

"Thus every feature I portray,
And color it a grewsome gray.
Half snake it seems, half dragon fell,
Spawned in some poisonous pool of Hell.
When thus its ghastly shape was wrought
A pair of bloodhounds fierce I sought,
Nimble and strong, and trained were they
The wild aurochs to make their prey.
These I incite to furious rage,
   And set them on their dragon foe,
Teaching them how the fight to wage,
   Till they my voice obedient know.

XII.

"And where the belly's tenderer skin
Allows sharp teeth to pierce within,
I urge them to attack it there,
With merciless fang to rend and tear,

While I bestride my Arab steed,
Sprung from the noblest, purest breed,
With spear in hand and spur on heel,
Kindling its rage with voice and steel,
Madly I urge its headlong course
  Full at the dragon's image fierce,
And cast my spear with utmost force,
    As though the monster to transpierce.

XIII.

"And though my charger wildly rears,
And champs, and foams with sudden fears,
And though my hounds with terror moan,
I rest not till they all have grown
Blunted with practice, day by day,
While thrice the moon renews her ray.
And when their training thus is o'er,
With them I seek our Island shore.
'Tis the third day since here I came :
  My eager limbs could know no rest,
Till the great deed had quenched the flame
    That burned resistless in my breast.

XIV.

" For the fresh griefs which filled the land
To hotter zeal my purpose fanned.

Some luckless hinds had lost their way
And mangled by the monster lay.
If in my heart a doubt could lurk,
'Twas past—I hastened to my work.
Briefly their duty I recount
To my brave squires: my horse I mount,
And with my noble leash of dogs,
   By hidden paths, which none may know,
Through silent marsh and trackless bogs,
   I fearless seek the hideous foe.

XV.

"The chapel, Lord, well knowest thou,
Hanging upon the mountain's brow,
O'erlooking all the Island round,
Which did our daring Master found.
Though mean it looks, and small and poor,
It shrines the source of many a cure,
The Mother with the Infant holy,
And the Three Kings adoring lowly.
Thrice thirty rock-hewn steps there lead
   The panting pilgrim to the height,
When wasted strength and dizzying head,
   Find fresh life in the Saviour's sight.

XVI.

" Deep in the rock, thus nobly crowned,
A noisome yawning cave is found,
Dank with the marsh's neighboring dews,
Where heaven's bright beams their light refuse.
'Twas here the hideous monster lay,
Waiting for victims, night and day;
Like Hell-drake keeping watch and ward,
The way to God's own house he barred :
For if, upon that dangerous path,
  The pious pilgrim careless went,
The monster rushed forth in his wrath,
  And limb from limb the victim rent.

XVII.

" To fit me for the doubtful fray,
Up the steep rock I bend my way,
To the Christ-child I kneel within
And cleanse my soul from taint of sin.
When I this holy state have won,
I draw my burnished armor on,
With spear in hand I quick descend,
Eager the bitter strife to end.
To a safe place my squires I bring,
  Briefly my last commands are given,

Upon my steed I lightly spring,
  While I commend my soul to Heaven.

XVIII.

" Scarcely the level plain I near,
Before my dogs give challenge clear.
With terror struck, my panting steed
Threatens to fail me in my need,
For, coil on coil, and close at hand
Lies the devourer of the land,
Basking beneath the blazing sun.
The nimble hounds towards him run.
But when he parts his ghastly jaw,
  And as his poisonous breath flies by,
They turn like arrows, filled with awe,
  And whimpering as the jackals cry.

XIX.

" Their courage quick I rouse again ;
Upon the foe they rush amain,
While at the monster's side is thrown
The spear with all the force I own.
But worthless as a reed it fails,
Rebounding from those steely scales ;

And ere a second cast is had,
My horse rears up, with terror mad,
That basilisk-eye he cannot face,
   Nor yet the monster's venom breath;
Beyond control, he backs apace,
    And all to me seems lost save death.

XX.

"Quick to the earth I leap, and there
In haste I lay my sword-edge bare,
But all my blows are spent in vain
That flinty mail to cleave in twain.
Raging it sweeps its tail around,
And hurls me helpless to the ground.
I see its grim throat yawning fierce,
Already seem its fangs to pierce—
But, wild with rage, my noble hounds
   Its belly rend with teeth and claws;
Loudly its bellowing resounds,
    As agony forces it to pause.

XXI.

"While from their grasp it vainly tries
To wrench itself, I swiftly rise,
I spy its vulnerable part,
And plunge my weapon in its heart;

Deep to the very hilt I bore—
Black-rushing spouts the monster's gore.
It falls, and with its mighty girth,
It bears me with it to the earth.
Bereft of sense, long time I lie,
  And when, at length, I rouse again,
My faithful squires are standing by
  The dragon in its life-blood slain."

XXII.

When ceased the knight, with briefest pause,
Burst forth the long restrained applause,
In that vast crowd, from every breast,
And echoing tenfold from the crest
Of the high vault, the mighty sound
Rolls thundering forth, below, around.
Even the Order's sons demand
A crown for him who freed the land.
Wildly the grateful people now
  In triumph forth the knight would bear:
But see, the Master knits his brow,
  And sternly orders silence there !

XXIII.

And speaks: "The dragon which this land
Laid waste, has fall'n 'neath thy brave hand.

A god the people think thee now :
To the Order but a foe art thou.
A reptile in thy heart hath lain
As evil as the one thou 'st slain.
The snake which tempts thy soul astray,
That leads us on destruction's way,
'Tis the rebellious spirit and high
   That thinks obedience little worth,
Sunders the law's most holy tie,
   And brings perdition upon earth.

XXIV.

"In valor shares the Paynim race :
Obedience is the Christian's grace.
For where our Saviour in his might,
Walked in the meekest, humblest plight,
Our sires, within that holy border,
Decreed the covenant of this Order—
The duty hardest to fulfil,
The effacement of our proper will.
But thee has idle glory stirred :
   Therefore betake thee from my sight.
Who beareth not the yoke o' the Lord
   Shall never with His cross be dight !"

XXV.

Then, through that vaulted chamber, loud
Storms forth the passion of the crowd :
For pardon all the brethren plead ;
But silently, with bended head,
The youth throws off his mantle, and
Kisses the Master's rigid hand.
Then goes—watched by the Master's eye,
Who calls him back with loving cry—
" My son, embrace me ; thou hast fought
    And won the nobler fight.   To thee
I give this cross, the guerdon bought
    By self-controlled humility !"

ULRICH VON HUTTEN'S COMPLAINT.

(From his refuge at Ufnau, in the Lake of Zurich, where he soon after
died, in 1523.)

NOT heedless did I dare it,
    No weak regret I feel ;
The gain, I may not share it,
    Yet none can doubt my zeal.
For all must own, not mine alone—
    The common good I favored,

Though now as the arch-enemy
   Of priests am I beslavered.

Well, let them deal in slander,
   And chatter as they will,
If I had but less candor,
   They had been gracious still.
For saying my say, I'm chased away,
   Of which complain I fairly.
No farther, though, than here I'll go,
   To return, mayhap, full early.

I will not sue for mercy,
   Since I no wrong have done:
The law's time-honored course I
   Had willingly let run.
But haste and spite and lawless might
   Refused me e'en a hearing.
And yet God's will must I fulfil,
   These heavy crosses bearing.

How oft hath such example
   Been witnessed in the past—
The strong, who sought to trample,
   Have lost the game at last!

A mighty flame from a spark oft came,
  So I revenge may take still.
The start is made, and with my aid,
  The cause must go or break still.

At least can I most truly
  Before the world assert
That ne'er those tongues unruly
  My honor dared to hurt.
Nor can they say that virtue's way
  I ever have forsaken,
Nor that with aught but righteous thought
  This cause have undertaken.

Will not our pious nation
  Resolve at length to cure,
As I wished, in thorough fashion,
  The wrongs it must endure?
Though sore I grieve, I take my leave—
  The cards I'll shuffle better.
All fearless I have cast the die—
  If Fate shall frown, why let her!

What though the courtiers' cunning
  May keep me anxious yet,
A heart, all evil shunning,
  Will hold its purpose set.

Full many I know to death who 'll go
   Our high designs to cherish—
Up horse and foot!   Come bravely to 't
   And let not Hutten perish!

AENNCHEN VON THARAU.

(SIMON DACH.)

ANNIE of Tharau, my heart's chiefest pleasure,
   She is my life and my hope and my treasure!
   Annie of Tharau in turn doth bestow
On me her heart, in its love and its wo.
Annie of Tharau, my wealth and my good!
Thou art my soul, and my flesh, and my blood!

Storms may beat on us from every hand,
We are resolved by each other to stand.
Sickness, injustice, misfortune, and pain
Only shall bind our loves closer again!
Annie of Tharau, my light and my sun,
Our lives shall encircle each other as one!

E'en as a palm-tree uprises again,
Bent though it hath been by storm-wind and rain,
So shall our love but new tenderness borrow
From the assaults of life's trouble and sorrow.
Annie of Tharau, my wealth and my good !
Thou art my soul, and my flesh, and my blood !

If thou shouldst from me be carried away,
Lived'st thou where man scarcely knows the sun's ray,
Thee would I follow through oceans and snows,
Iron and prison, and armies of foes.
Annie of Tharau, my light and my sun,
Our lives shall encircle each other as one !

DE CONTEMPTU MUNDI.

[There is perhaps no more thorough embodiment of the medieval monas-
tic theory of life and death than the poem from which the following
fragments are translated. A portion of it has been attributed to
St. Bernard, probably from its similarity to the Dies Iræ, which is
likewise sometimes ascribed to him.]

AH mortal life ! so false and brief,
    Why cast seductions thus o'er me ?
    Since thou must fall, as falls the leaf,
    Why force me thus to cling to thee ?

Ah mortal life that swiftly flies,
  More evil than the tiger's brood,
Since I so soon must rend thy ties,
  Why lead'st thou thus my soul from good?

Ah life—nay, rather death thou art—
  A thing for hate and not for love,
Since evil only is thy part,
  Why dost thou thus my senses move?

Ah life, full-fraught with sickly fears,
  More fragile than the tenderest flower,
Since thou art weighted thus with tears,
  Why own I thy alluring power?

Ah life, that knows nor peace nor rest,
  In troubled thought and anxious heart,
Wearying with endless, aimless quest,
  Why do I grieve that we must part?

*   *   *   *   *   *

Whene'er on death's approach I dwell,
  And all the terrors in his train,
Appalled I shrink, for who can tell
  If he may 'scape Hell's endless pain?

Appalled, the dreadful Day I wait,
  The Day of grief and voiceless gloom,
The Day of wrath and pitiless fate,
  The Day that wreaks the sinner's doom.

I shudder when I think of Him
  Who knows the heart's most secret thought,
The terrible Judge who comes supreme
  To avenge each sin by mortal wrought.

For who without dismay shall stand
  Before that awful Presence, where
The quenchless fires on either hand
  The sinner's hopeless fate prepare?

*   *   *   *   *   *

How sweet for him 'twill be, how blest,
  Who hath the world's allurements spurned!
What sharp despair for him whose breast
  For worldly hopes and joys hath yearned!

Hail, blessed ones, who weep and mourn,
  Who suffer for the Saviour here!
For you the world's unrest and scorn
  Shall gain a lasting kingdom there.

Where hate and fear will be unknown,
  Whence sorrow will be banished far,
With want, and age's palsied moan,
  And all that perfect bliss could mar.

There peace will fold her wings and stay,
  There gladness will unsullied be,
There youth will never feel decay,
  And health will dread no enemy.

'Twere vain to strive in words to tell
  The exulting, boundless rapture given
To those who thus on high shall dwell
  And reign with angel hosts in heaven.

O hearken to my earnest prayer,
  Great Judge! and call me to Thy side.
This is my hope, my chiefest care,
  Let not Thy servant be denied! Amen!

DIES IRÆ.

O DAY of wrath! O day, foretold
By God's own chosen seers of old,
Which shall the world in flames enfold!

What fear upon mankind shall fall
When the Great Judge shall come, and all
To His strict judgment-seat shall call!

The wondrous trump's mysterious tone
Shall pierce the fields which Death has sown,
And force all sinners to the Throne.

For Death astonied then shall be,
While Nature sets her creatures free,
To wait the Judge's stern decree.

Then forth shall be the record brought,
Of every deed and every thought,
From which the judgment shall be wrought.

And when the Judge his seat has ta'en,
All hidden things shall be made plain,
And naught shall unavenged remain.

Then what defence can such as I
Put forth?   On what protector cry,
When scarce the just can hope descry?

O King of awful majesty,
The chosen ones are saved by Thee!
Then, Font of Mercy, save Thou me!

Sweet Christ! on that day spurn me not!
For me, I pray, remember what
Thou borest in Thine earthly lot!

Me didst Thou seek, in care and pain;
For me upon the Cross wast slain;
Let not Thy sufferings be in vain!

Thou righteous Judge of retribution,
Grant, O grant me absolution,
Ere the day of prosecution!

All self-condemned I scarce can speak;
The blush of shame o'erspreads my cheek;
God! grant the pardon that I seek!

Thou, who sad Mary hast forgiven,
Thou, who the dying thief hast shriven,
Thou givest me also hope of heaven.

Worthless my prayers, I own with shame,
But, Blest One, let Thy holy Name
Preserve me from the endless flame!

Amid the sheep, O bid me stand,
Far from the goats' unhallowed band,
And place me safe at Thy right hand!

When the accursed shall hear the knell
That dooms them to the fires of Hell,
Call me among the blest to dwell!

With contrite heart I lowly bend,
Before Thee, praying Thee to send
To all my fears a blessed end!

Ah! tearful well may be that day
When man shall rise from earthly clay,
To meet the Law's avenging rod—
Then spare me! spare me, O my God!

DRINKING SONG.

[Attributed to WALTER DE MAPES, Archdeacon of Oxford at the close of the twelfth century.]

IN a cosey tavern am I resolved to die,
  Drinking still, and drinking, forever as I lie,
  That the angel chorus on seeing me may cry,
  "God, take this stout drinker in peace beyond the sky!"

Nerved with deep potations, wit kindleth fast its fires;
Strengthened with the grape-juice, the heart to heaven as-
    pires;
Strong draughts in the taverns my thirsty soul desires
More than the weak mixtures they give us at the 'Squire's.

Nature hath for each one some gift to serve him ever.
When I'm dry and empty, then I can scribble never.
Fasting, I'll be beaten by any boy that's clever.
Thirst I hate, and hunger, as Styx's muddy river.

At his birth to each man some gift kind Nature bore.
With the fairest wine I the Muses' aid implore,
For it is well known that the vintner's sparkling store
Brings a flood of fancies, and words in mighty roar.

Changeful are my verses, they vary with my wine.
I make no pretension to write well till I dine.
Poems made when empty are stupid, every line,
But, on three good bumpers, I'll Ovid far outshine.

The prophetic power within me all is vain
Till my well-filled stomach hath made my doublet strain,
Then when Bacchus mounteth and whirleth through my
    brain,
Phœbus rusheth in me, and makes all wonders plain!

EPITAPH.

(MARTIAL.)

LIGHT be the turf that veils thy tender head,
O Alcimus! Alas, too early dead!
Upon thy grave no ponderous tomb shall be
Of perishing dust an empty mockery;
But where thou liest shall fragrant flowers be laid,
And twining boughs shall cast a solemn shade.
And oft my tears, like Heaven's own springing dew,
In summer's heat shall make them bloom anew.
Do not these tributes of my grief disdain—
Here, through all time, thy memory shall remain,
And when the stern Fates shall my death decree,
In dust will I be joined again to thee!

THE VOW.

(TIBULLUS.)

NO other love shall e'er beguile
   My once too wandering heart from thee,
For thou 'rt the first whose winning smile
   Hath made it feel what love should be.

No other form can charm my eyes—
   Ah, would that mine were charmed alone !
That none might crave my heart's own prize,
   For thou wouldst then be all mine own !

For the envying gaze I do not care
   Of jealous youths. Thy secret love
Might well repay me to forbear
   The fame that I thy heart could move.

Thus could I live most blissfully
   With thee, embowered in forest glades,
Where foot of man we ne'er should see
   Intruding on our sacred shades.

And thou shouldst be my balm in care,
   In my dark night the guiding star,
My world, my all—whence I with fear
   Would view the whirl of life afar.

And now, though heaven itself should send
  To me another, fair as day,
To her my heart should never bend
  From thee, whom it shall love alway.

I swear it by the Queen of Heaven,
  Juno, the first of gods to me—
Fool that I am! I now have given
  Irrevocably myself to thee I

Unthinkingly I swore, alas!
  'Twas fear that did betray me so,
And now wilt thou scorn him who has
  No way to 'scape from thee and woe.

I am thy slave and must obey,
  Nor seek to rive my cruel chain—
Yet I to Venus oft will pray,
  Who never hears my prayers in vain!

TO ARISTIAS FUSCUS.

(HORACE.)

FUSCUS, the man whose life is pure,
    Who shuns foul evil's devious arts,
  Needs not the javelin of the Moor,
    Nor poisoned darts,

Whether by Afric's burning shore,
  Or mid Caucasian snows, or where
Hydaspes flows o'er fabled ore,
    His way may fare.

For late as 'neath the woodland shade,
  Wandering I sang of Lalage,
Careless and all unarmed, there fled
    A wolf from me!

And such a monster! Daunias ne'er
  His like in her dark forests nursed,
Nor Mauritania, savage lair
    Of beasts accursed.

Then were I borne to that dull waste
  Which genial summer never warms,
By grateful verdure never graced,
    Mid clouds and storms;

Or to those lifeless Southern isles,
    Too near the sun's relentless rays,
I 'd still love Lalage's bright smiles,
    And winsome ways.

TO TORQUATUS.

(HORACE.)

THE snows have fled; the fields again are blooming;
    To life the trees have sprung;
No longer o'er their banks the brooks are spuming,
    And Earth once more is young.
Now may the Nymphs and Graces, in their bower,
    Their naked dances weave.
To us the circling year, each passing hour,
    Life's mortal lesson give.
Mild Zephyrs melt the frost: Spring yields to Summer,
    And Summer dies when Fall
Pours forth her fruitage; then the latest comer,
    Dull Winter, endeth all.
The year's decay, the moons revolving o'er us
    Will soon make good; but we,

When we rejoin those who have gone before us,
    But dust and shades shall be !
Who knows if to his day a single morrow
    Will be decreed by Fate?
The wealth that thou hast heaped, through joy and sorrow,
    Thy heir will dissipate.
When death, Torquatus, comes, and Minos o'er thee
    His dread award shall give,
Not thy high birth, nor eloquence shall restore thee,
    Nor piety bid thee live.
Hippolytus from Styx e'en Dian never
    To earth could bring again,
Nor for Pirithous could Theseus sever
    Lethe's unyielding chain.

THE DYING HADRIAN'S ADDRESS TO HIS SOUL.

THOU playful wandering sprite,
    This body's comrade-guest,
Whither is now thy flight,
Naked, and cold, and white,
    And never more to jest?

LINES.

SUGGESTED BY A FRAGMENT OF ALCÆUS.

Μηδὲν ἀλλο φυτεύσης πρότερον δένδρεον ἀμπέλω.

L ET nothing but the fruitful vine
  Be planted near this house of mine ;
  But it shall twine luxuriant o'er
  And ripely cluster round the door,
As if to say " None enter here
Save those to whom the vine is dear !"

And so 'twill be. No friend I'll own
Save those who love the vine alone.
And they, a chosen few, shall meet
Beneath the vine-tree's foliage sweet,
Whose clusters, hanging high, shall beam,
Reflected in the purple stream.

I've striven for all that Earth can give,
For which is man content to live,
And I have found that, once possessed,
There's naught that fills the craving breast.
From each new joy the heart flies fleeter,
And still it asks for something sweeter.

I've basked an hour in Beauty's smile,
And then have scorned the plaything's wile.

For love is but an endless round
Of causeless sighs and bliss unfound.
The myrtle's frail and barren flower
Is fitting emblem of its power.

And I, for Fame, have pondered o'er
The sage's legendary lore.
I've sought her with my brand and shield,
And wooed her in the stricken field.
Yon faded laurel wreath can tell
How she rewards her votaries well!

No! I care not for Beauty's eyes—
My love within the goblet lies.
I care not for the voice of Fame,
While I can breathe the goblet's flame.
Then plant alone the fruitful vine
Around this humble home of mine!

THE SWALLOWS.

(AGATHIAS THE MYRENÆAN.)

THE weary night I spend in sighs
  Of hopeless love, and bitter tears ;
And sleep begins to seal my eyes
  Just as the rosy dawn appears.
But as, in sweet forgetfulness,
  My heart begins to find relief,
Ye call my soul from dreams that bless,
  Ye clamorous swallows, back to grief !

Ah then ye envious chatterers cease!
  It was not I who wronged the maid—
I broke not Philomela's peace—
  By guiltier hands was she betrayed.
For Itys do ye grieve? Away!
  Go seek the mountain's lonely height,
And there pour forth your mournful lay
  From earliest dawn to blackest night ;

Or in some desert wild, where none
  Are near whom your discordant cries
Can rouse. Perchance when ye are gone
  Slumber again may press my eyes.

And even in some rapturous dream,
   Some vision fraught with wildering charms,
I may be blest, until I deem
   I rest within Rhodanthe's arms!

THE FREEBOOTER.

(HYBRIAS THE CRETAN.)

HERE is my wealth!   A falchion bright,
   A spear, a shield with bull-skin dight,
   Protecting me through many a fight,
     While swords are flashing round!

Through these the harvest all is mine,
And vintage, red with spouting wine,
While slaves, with terror struck, incline,
     Before me, to the ground!

But they who wield no falchion bright,
Nor spear, nor shield with bull-skin dight
Protecting them through many a fight,
     While swords are flashing round—

Yea, all such craven sons of fear
Shall humbly bend to me, where'er
I go, and me as Lord revere—
     Their Lord and King uncrowned!

BION'S THIRD IDYLL.

———

'TWAS a sweet dream !   Cythera stood before me,
  And in her hand did she young Eros bring;
  And thus she spoke, while bending gracefully o'er me—
    "Shepherd, teach him thy honeyed strains to sing,
And glad my soul !"   With this sweet task delighted,
  Blindly I welcomed the deceiver, Love,
And strove to teach him the soft chants recited
  For ages by the shepherds of the grove.
The legends old which tell how Pan invented
  The shrilly pipes, Athena her sweet flute,
How Hermes with his lyre the list augmented,
  And bright Apollo framed the melting lute.
When I had done, I gave to him the lyre,
  But he neglected all the strains I taught,
And straight sang little songs of fierce desire,
  Relating deeds by his dear mother wrought—
The strange wild tales of all the gods of Heaven,
  Who in their bosoms oft felt passion's swell.
For my own lays I care not since that even,
  But those he taught, I know them but too well !

HYMN TO ZEUS.

(CLEANTHES.)

[Classic antiquity has left us few passages more elevated in thought
and feeling than this fragment of Cleanthes, the disciple and suc-
cessor of Zeno, founder of the Stoic philosophy. In its virtual
monotheism, and in its conceptions of the relations between good
and evil, it anticipates much later speculation.]

FIRST of immortals, ever-reigning Zeus,
 Invoked by many names, all hail to Thee,
 The great Creator, who dost govern all things
 With never-failing justice!   Thus I lift
My voice to Thee, for Thou dost graciously
To mortals lend thine ear.   The power of speech,
To man alone of all that walk the earth,
Thou givest, for Thou his heavenly Father art,
And he can pray to Thee—a priceless boon!
Thy praise shall ever be my theme; Thy power
And goodness be the burden of my thought.

The universe which round the earth is rolled
In all obeys Thee, and by Thee is ruled;
And in Thy mighty hand the lightning bolt
Is but an instrument to work Thy will—
Dread minister before whom Nature trembles!
But Thou dost guide it with the unerring law

Which throughout all creation rules the spheres,
Linking the greater and the lesser orbs.

Naught happens upon earth save through Thy will,
Or 'mid the ocean's dark abodes, or in
The starry firmament of heaven.   And though
The senseless deeds of evil men might seem
To make against Thy justice, yet Thou hast
The might to balance all things.   Thus through Thee
Order from chaos springs and good from evil.
For in Thy wisdom Thou hast blended so
The good with ill, that there arises one
Law universal, from whose measureless bonds
The things of ill strive vainly to escape.
So they whose darkened souls cannot descry
Thy wisdom's fateful force, or recognize
The high reward of calm obedience—
They blindly with each other still contend,
Some seeking fame, laborious to win,
Yet leaving ever a void within the heart,
That wastes itself in the pursuit; and some
For gain themselves debasing, rendering up
Their very souls to avarice ; others rushing
Blindly to madness, or abandoning
Themselves to the allurements of the senses :
And nearing thus, by all these devious paths,

The common goal of evil, each one sees
The prize he labored for elude his grasp,
Even as he hoped to snatch it, and instead
He finds his punishment in what he longed for.

Then, Zeus, all bounteous, ruler of high heaven,
Dispel the baleful ignorance which beclouds
The soul of man! Give him to understand
That only real wisdom with which Thou
Dost guide the universe! In that supreme
And perfect knowledge, he at last will learn
How Thee to honor, and Thy might to praise.
Nor men nor gods can better spend themselves
Than praising Wisdom's rule as shown in Thee!

GUARINOS.

(ROMANCERO CASTELLANO.)

[The most popular of the Spanish ballads of the Carlovingian cycle. It is the melancholy song chanted by the peasant and overheard by Don Quijote, P. II. ch. ix.]

IT fared ill with you, ye Franks, in the Roncesvalles fray,
    When your Charles fled in dishonor, while his twelve
        peers dying lay!
It was there they took Guarinos, the Frankish admiral,
Seven Moorish kings together, who each claimed him
    for his thrall.

Seven times the lot they threw, and all seven times it fell
To Marlotes the Infante, the proud arch infidel.
And Marlotes prized it higher than all the Arab land,
And he spake thus to the captive, who stood at his right
    hand.

"In Allah's name I bid thee, Guarinos, to turn Moor,
And of riches and of honors I will give thee ample store.
Behold I have two daughters, two maidens fair to see,
Both of them shall be thine, for both will I give to thee.

"The one to tend thy raiment, and to work thy jewelled
    shoon;
The other, she shall be thy wife ere wanes yon crescent
    moon,
And with her, as her dower, the whole of Araby—
And speak if more thou wantest, for yet more I'll give to
    thee."

Then answered bold Guarinos, "May Jesus work me scathe,
And His Mother, Holy Mary, if I forsake His faith!
If I forsake His faith for the lies of false Mahoun!
And my lady love in France, I will wed with her alone!"

To a dungeon dark and noisome Guarinos then was ta'en,
With thick fetters on his hands, that he ne'er should fight
    again,
With water to his girdle, that he ne'er again should ride,
And of iron seven quintals were fastened to his side.
And at Pentecost and Christmas and at the Easter-tide,
With cruel stripes thrice yearly, they scourged him in their
    pride.

The days they come, the days they go, to the day of good
    St. John,
Which Christian, Jew, and Moslem, all keep in unison,
When Christians scatter rushes, when Moors sweet myrtle lay,
And Jews strew blooming vetches, in honor of the day.

To aid in the rejoicing, Marlotes built on high
A target-frame so lofty that it seemed to pierce the sky.
With laughing zeal the Moslem their lances at it cast,
But all in vain, for none had skill to reach a height so vast.

In sullen wrath Marlotes proclaimed with trumpet sound,
" No babe shall suck, no man shall eat, till the targe lies on
 the ground !"
Guarinos heard the shouting in his dungeon dark and drear—
"Now help me, God in heaven, and His Holy Mother dear,
Marlotes' daughter surely hath now her bridal cheer,
Or 'tis the day of scourging, I had not thought so near."

Then answered him the gaoler, who had heard him thus
 complain,
" This is not a royal bridal, nor thy day of stripes and pain,
But the feast of good St. John, which of all days in the year
Is the blithest and the merriest, with sports and royal cheer.

"And to aid in the rejoicing hath Marlotes built on high
A target-frame so lofty that it seems to pierce the sky,
But the Moors have failed to reach it, and the king's stern
 word goes round,
No babe shall suck, no man shall eat, till the targe lies on
 the ground !"

Then to him spake Guarinos, his words I truly tell,
"If ye'll give me back my charger, who once carried me
    so well,
And give me back my armor, and the lance I wont to bear,
Then I that lofty target to overthrow will dare,
If I fail my head is forfeit, and my blood ye need not spare!''

The wondering gaoler answered, " 'Tis seven full years that
    here,
Yea seven, thou'st lain where no man I thought could live
    a year,
And yet this feat to venture thou deem'st not overbold!
Have patience but a little, and Marlotes shall be told."

To Marlotes near the target the gaoler ran with speed—
"Strange news I bring, O listen, and graciously give heed.
Guarinos boasts thy target he will shiver high in air,
If thou his steed wilt give him, and the arms he wont to
    bear."

Marlotes listened wondering, then, swelling in his pride,
He bade them fetch Guarinos, to see if he could ride,
And bade them seek his charger, which, through all that
    weary time,
Had spent his noble vigor in daily hauling lime.

They put his armor on him, with rust all deeply worn ;
Marlotes when he saw him, with jibes and cruel scorn,
Bade him to strike the target and fell it to the ground.
In fiery wrath Guarinos rushed forward with a bound,
And at the first cast full one-half fell down with thundering
sound.

The Moors enraged flew at him and sought to slay him there,
In multitudes so countless that they darkened all the air.
Like a good knight Guarinos his trusty sword laid bare,
And clove through mail and turban with a strength beyond
compare.

Through all that furious melley his way he cut amain,
And onward pricked his charger, nor ever drew the rein
Till far away behind him lay the distant hills of Spain.
And glad enow were the Franks, I trow, to welcome him
again!

THE DEATH OF THE CID.

(ROMANCERO DEL CID.)

I.

IN his good town of Valencia lay the Cid, all spent and
worn
    With the battles he had won and with the labors he had
borne,
When to him tidings came which well might give him anxious care,
For Bucar the Great was on the march in hopes to meet him
there,
With thirty kings in his array, and horse and foot to spare.

Upon his couch Rodrigo tossed, in earnest thought and
prayer
That God to him in desperate strait would timely succor
bear,
When suddenly at his bedside the good Cid was aware
Of a man with shining countenance and snow-white, lustrous
hair.

"Art thou asleep?" the Figure spake "If so, arouse and
list!"
"And who art thou," the Cid replied, "who makest such
request?"

"St. Peter am I called, the chief of the Apostolate,
And I come to cheer thee in thy care, and read to thee thy
    fate.

" But thirty days of life hast thou upon this earth to spend,
For God hath called thee up to Heaven, to the life that hath
    no end ;
And in His love He granteth thee a special grace, for
    know
That, after death, this proud Bucar thou shalt meet and over-
    throw.

"With all his vast array thy men shall meet him in the
    field,
And with Santiago's good help shall make the Paynim yield.
But thou, Rodrigo Campeador, for thy sins make amends,
And fit thee for that heavenly life which God in mercy
    sends.

"All this doth God through love of me, in recompense of
    thine
Assiduous service rendered me at famed Cardeña's shrine."
The good Cid much rejoicing leaped from off the bed to
    greet
Upon his knees the Apostle, and to kiss his holy feet.

But Peter said, " In vain thou triest my form to touch, yet
    hold
As certain truth the things which I this night to thee have
    told;"
Then rose to Heaven, and left the Cid of all his cares con-
    soled,
And giving heartfelt thanks to God, with spirit high and bold.

II.

The good Cid of Vibar lies dead, released from mortal ills.
His trusty henchman, Gil Diaz, his last command fulfils:
The corpse embalmed, with open eyes, and cheeks with color
    rife,
With beard and hair arranged with care, as he was wont in
    life,
Looks all so fair as though he were now ready for the strife.

With artful cunning Gil Diaz, to make it upright rest,
Has placed it sitting in a chair, with a board against the
    breast,
And another fastened to the back, the two together tied
So deftly that the head erect can sway to neither side.

'Tis twelve days since Rodrigo's soul to Heaven has passed
    away,
And now his men are all arrayed and eager for the fray,

To sally forth as Christians should, with axe and lance and
    sword,
To meet the King Bucar and all his misbelieving horde.

At dead of night the corpse is brought, and to the saddle-bow
Of Bavieca, his good steed, they bind it fast enow,
So that it firmly sits upright, as he alive were there,
With hosen wrought in black and white, like the greaves he
    used to wear.

Around the neck his shield is hung, with all his arms dis-
    played,
And a parchment casque that looks like steel, upon the head
    is laid ;
And Tizona, his own true sword, is poised in the right hand,
Uplifted high, as though to chase the Moslem from his land.
The Bishop, Don Geronimo, on one side closely rides,
While on the other Gil Diaz proud Bavieca guides.

Pedro Bermudez, bearing the Cid's banner, leads the van,
With four hundred as its guardians, each a gallant gentleman.
Then comes the main array, each one a man of pith and
    might,
With four hundred gallant gentlemen to lead them in the
    fight.

And next the body of the Cid, with a picked and chosen
band
Of a hundred valiant cavaliers, who ride on either hand.
Doña Ximena follows last, with all her lovely train—
Six hundred knights in that sweet charge all gently draw the
rein.

At break of day they draw away from old Valencia's walls.
Alvar Fañez with fury first upon the Moslem falls.
Right in his front Estrella stands—a Mooress famed was she
Throughout all Islam for her wondrous skill in archery.

With Turkish bow and poisoned reeds she slays men from
afar,
Like to some baleful planet, whence the name she bears—
the Star:
With hundred comrades now she leads the army of Bucar.
But the Christians charge so fiercely that they all lie slaugh-
tered there,
While Bucar and all his thirty kings are palsied with despair.

For seventy thousand cavaliers, all white as snow, they see,
Bearing down on them in the van of the Christian chivalry,
With one who rides a charger white, more dreadful than the
rest,
Of stately port, who wears a blood-red cross upon his breast;

A banner white he waves on high, and with a sword that
    shines
Like living fire he scatters dire destruction through their
    lines.

Bucar and all his thirty kings rush headlong from the fray,
And hurry to the neighboring shore, where his proud navy
    lay.
The Cid's men follow, slaughtering fast, and drive them in
    the sea,
And full ten thousand there are drowned in vain attempt
    to flee.

Bucar escapes, but twenty kings lie stretched upon the plain,
While the Christians spoil the Moslem camp and therein find
    much gain,
In piles of gold and silver, with rich plate and jewels rare —
Were none so poor but now are rich, as they that booty
    share.

Then as the good Cid had ordained, that noble funeral train
Resumes its march through fair Castile unto St. Peter's fane,
At famed Cardeña, where they weep to lay him in the grave
Whom Spain shall ever honor as the bravest of the brave!

MOORISH BALLAD.

Sung previous to the rising of the Moriscos in 1568.

[The first confirmation of the rumors of the Morisco rebellion was de-
rived from a Spanish translation of this ballad, sent with an inter-
cepted letter by the Marques de Mondejar to Philip II. in 1568
(Marmol, Hist. del Rebelion y Castigo de los Moros, III. ix.). It
derives interest from its elevated conceptions of God, its hearty con-
tempt for the less simple Catholic theology and ritual, and its vivid
picture of persecution endured.]

LET the God of love and mercy's name begin and end
    our theme—
    Sovereign He o'er all the nations, of all things the
    Judge Supreme:
He who gave the book of wisdom, He who made His image,
    man,
He chastiseth, He forgiveth, He who framed creation's plan.

He the One sole God of Heaven, He the One sole God of
    earth,
He who guards us and supports us, He from whom all things
    had birth;
He who never had beginning, sovereign Lord of the high
    throne,
He whose providence guides all things, subject to His will
    alone.

He who gave us Holy Scripture, who made Adam, and who
    planned

Man's salvation, He who gives their strength to nations from
    His hand ;

He who raised the Saints and Prophets, ending with Mahoun
    the greatest—

Praise the One sole God of Heaven, with all His Saints, from
    first to latest !

Listen, while I tell the story of Andalusia's fate—

Peerless once and world-renowned in all that makes a nation
    great ;

Prostrate now and compassed round by heretics with cruel
    force—

We, her sons, like driven sheep, or horseman on unbridled
    horse.

Torture is our daily portion, subtle craft our sole resource,

Till we welcome death to free us from a fate that 's ever
    worse.

They have set the Jews to watch us, Jews that know nor
    truth nor faith,

Every day they find some new device to work us further
    scathe.

We are forced to worship with them in their Christian rites
    unclean,
To adore their painted idols, mockery of the Great Unseen.
No one dares to make remonstrance, no one dares to speak
    a word ;
Who can tell the anguish wrought on us, the faithful of the
    Lord ?

When the bell tolls, we must gather to adore the image foul ;
In the church the preacher rises, harsh-voiced as a scream-
    ing owl ;
He the wine and pork invoketh, and the Mass is wrought
    with wine ;
Falsely humble, he proclaimeth that this is the Law divine.

Yet the holiest of their shavelings nothing knows of right or
    wrong,
And they bow before their idols, shameless in the shameless
    throng.
Then the priest ascends the altar, holding up a cake of
    bread,
And the people strike their bosoms as the worthless Mass is
    said.

All our names are set in writing, young and old are sum-
    moned all ;
Every four months the official makes on all suspect his call.

7

Each of us must show his permit, or must pay his silver o'er,
As with inkhorn, pen, and paper, on he goes from door to
door.
Dead or living, each must pay it ; young or old, or rich or
poor ;
God help him who cannot do it, pains untold he must endure !

They have framed a false religion ; idols sitting they adore ;
Seven weeks fast they, like the oxen who at noon-tide eat the
more.
In the priest and the confession they their baseless law fulfil,
And we, too, must feign believing, lest they do us further
ill.

Toil they spare not to entrap us, day and night, and far and
near,
Whoso praises God aloud cannot escape destruction here.
Vain were hiding, vain were flight, when once the spies are
on his track,
Should he gain a thousand leagues, they follow him and
bring him back.

In their hideous jails they throw him, every hour fresh terrors weave,
From his ancient faith to tear him, as they cry to him " Believe !"

And the poor wretch, weeping, wanders on from hopeless
    thought to thought,
Like a swimmer in mid ocean, by the blinding tempest
    caught.

Long they keep him wasting, rotting, in the dungeon foul
    and black,
Then they torture him until his limbs are broken on the rack,
Then within the Plaza Hatabin the crowds assemble fast,
Like unto the Day of Judgment they erect a scaffold vast.
If one is to be released, they clothe him in a yellow vest,
While with hideous painted devils to the flames they give the
    rest.

Thus are we encompassed round as with a fiercely burning
    fire,
Wrongs past bearing are heaped on us, higher yet and ever
    higher.
Vainly bend we to their mandates; Sundays, feast-days
    though we keep,
Fasting Saturdays and Fridays, never safety can we reap.

Each one of their petty despots thinks that he can make the
    law,
Each invents some new oppression. Now a sharper sword
    they draw!

New Year's day in Bib-el-Bonut they proclaimed some edicts
  new,
Startling sleepers from their slumbers, as each door they
  open threw.

Baths and garments, all our old ancestral customs are for-
  bidden,
To the Jews are we delivered, who can spoil us still un-
  chidden.
Little reck the priest and friar so they trample on us yet ;
Like a dove in vulture talons, we are more and more beset.

Hopeless, then, of man's assistance, we have searched the
  prophets o'er,
Seeking promise in the judgments which our fathers writ of
  yore ;
And our wise men counsel us to look to God with prayer
  and fast—
Haply through fresh suffering will He deliver us at last !

I have done ; but life were short our sorrows fully to recall.
Kind Señores, do not blame me, if I am too weak for all.
Whoso chants these rugged verses, let his prayers to God
  arise,
That His mercy may vouchsafe me the repose of Paradise !

DANTE.

(MICHELANGELO.)

THROUGH blind abysmal depths he plunged, and there
He viewed the twin abodes of souls in pain :
Then rose to God, returned to earth again,
And taught the truths that he alone could dare.

A brilliant star, his rays of lustre rare
Revealed to man the dim, eternal reign.
And his the portion which the world profane
Is wont to make its chiefest heroes share.

For Dante's noble toil and purpose high
Met foul return from that ungrateful herd,
Withholding favor only from the good.
Were I but such! Might I such fate but try!
Earth's costliest gifts I'd hold in slight regard
To gain his exile with his lofty mood!

LAURA.

(PETRARCH)

WHEN Love seems lurking in each radiant face
  Of these fair girls, my senses to enthrall,
  So much as she is fairer than them all,
So much the more my passion grows apace.
And then I bless the time, the hour, the place,
  When first on her my glances dared to fall:
  And gratefully upon my soul I call
"Give thanks that thou hast won so rare a grace—
That holy love for which thou long hast striven,
  Lifting the faithful heart to realms above,
  Disdaining all that common mortals love,
  And strengthening in thee the resolves which move
Thee still to labor on thy way to heaven!"
And thus to me a nobler life is given!

DE PROFUNDIS.

W E are born, we know not why,
    We toil, through want and care;
    Worn out, at last we die,
    And go, we know not where.

We suffer, we inflict,
    Unknowing what we do:
We gain, to find us tricked;
    We lose, to idly rue.

If the soul, impatient, aims
    At something higher, better,
The flesh asserts its claims,
    And will not loose its fetter.

Nor Hindu sage, nor Greek
    Can aid our impotence:
The highest goal they seek
    Is dumb indifference.

The Christian's nobler plan
　　But palliates the ill :
All man can do for man
　　Leaves Earth in misery still.

The riddle who can read ?
　　Who guess the reason why?
We know but this, indeed,
　　We are born, we grieve, we die !

THE NATION'S TRIAL.　(1861.)

O Romagnuoli, tornati in bastardi.—Purgat. xvi.

SWORD of our fathers !　In the sheath
　　Through long years hast thou idly lain.
Now with firm hand and reverent faith
　　We sternly draw thee forth again.

Strange human heart, that turns to gall
　　God's choicest fruits !　To us were given
Kind Nature, wondrous Science, all
　　That man can ask of earth or heaven.

But lust of gain, and selfish greed
   Of vulgar power and empty show
Have weighed us down, till thought and deed
   Centre on sordid aims and low.

Corrupted by this earthly stain
   Our souls have lost their nobler guise,
And now we feel the fiery rain
   Which or destroys or purifies.

God grant that we have something still
   Of that stern stuff which bore our sires
Unshrinkingly through good and ill,
   That we may stand those ordeal-fires.

Then, Sword, leap forth, and in the strife
   Shall those foul stains be hewn away.
High thoughts, high deeds, a nobler life
   Our agony shall well repay!

THE HOLOCAUST. (1861.)

"Their silver and their gold shall not be able to deliver them in the day of the wrath of the Lord."—Ezekiel vii.

WITHIN our country's sacred fane,
   Low burns the altar's flickering light.
  Trembling we watch it slowly wane—
   That lost, what star shall guide our night?

Then gather round that holy flame
  And bring your choicest offerings here.
What dearest victims can ye name,
  For such a sacrifice too dear?

Pour forth your blood, pile up your gold—
  'Tis well—but more than these we need.
No nation's life is bought and sold,
  Nor saved alone by valorous deed.

Then here your cherished vices bring:
  Your luxury's degrading ease;
The reckless pride with which ye cling
  To wealth's most abject vanities;

Your worship of successful fraud;
  Your want of faith in nobler aims;

Your blind self-seeking, and the broad
　　Ignoring of all loftier claims;

Your partisanship which beguiles
　　To faction's aid its clamorous tools;
Your apathy, which feebly smiles
　　When power is clutched by knaves and fools.

Come, offer in our solemn rite
　　Each sordid vice and base desire;
Rise up in manhood's simple might,
　　And naught shall quench our altar's fire!

THE ARMIES OF THE UNION. (1861.)

FROM Maine's deep-wooded hills to far Pacific's Golden
　　　Gate,
　　They gather to the battle, like the answering step of
　　fate.
They ask not who their leaders be, they only know the cause:
Old feuds are hushed as each one round the sacred banner
　　draws.

They come not here to plunder foes, they are not urged by
hate,
Nor lured by hopes of conquest, or Ambition's glittering
bait.
No conscripts they, constrained to fight at any master's nod,
But each a freeman proud who bows the knee to only God.

Each claims the nation as a whole, from distant shore to
shore,
To each belongs the starry flag his fathers raised of yore,
And each has sworn no rebel knave shall rend the land in
twain,
Or blot one star from off that flag, so long without a stain.

Sprung from a martial race are they, yet peaceful toils alone,
In building up an empire vast, their sturdy hands have
known,
But now the plough, the loom, the pen are sternly cast aside,
As the Nation rises in its wrath to cast down treason's pride.

Full many a soldier's grave there 'll be, full many a darkened home,
Where wife and mother sickening wait for him who ne'er
shall come,
Yet for each one who nobly falls another stands prepared,
To take his place, to wield his arms, and dare all he had
dared.

If fate should frown, and treason's flag, o'er many a stricken
    field
Should proudly flaunt, theirs is a blood that knows not how
    to yield;
For gathering strength with each reverse, those stubborn
    bands would grow,
As the torrent swells against the rocks that vainly check its
    flow.

Oh could they fail, man's hopes would fail of freedom ever-
    more!
The peaceful reign of unarmed law and equal rights were
    o'er.
Then close your lines and strike home deep amid the traitor
    clan—
No nobler cause the world has seen since man first warred
    with man.

THE LESSON OF WAR. (1861.)

ex est, non poena, perire.—MARTIAL.

WILD warriors of the past, whose flashing swords
    Light up with fitful gleams the misty night
Of half-forgotten eld, in fiery words,
    Ye teach a truth 'twere well we read aright.

God sends the gentle breeze to woo the flower,
    And stir the pulses of the ripening corn.
He, too, lets loose the whirlwind's vengeful power,
    To quench the plagues of foul stagnation born.

And thus in love, although disguised as wrath,
    He sends His hidden blessings in the storm,
Which dashes down, on its resistless path,
    The hoar abuses that defied reform.

When Cyrus ravaged fair Chaldæa's plain
    And mocked the strength of Babylon's haughty wall,
The proud Assyrian's guilt had earned the chain,
    And man rejoiced to mark the oppressor's fall.

And when, made drunk with power, the Persian lost
    The stern and simple virtues of his race,
His baffled efforts and his slaughtered host
    Enriched the world with Grecian power and grace.

Then Greece, her swift career of glory stayed,
  Exhausted by her madman's triumphs lay,
Till Rome's protecting arm the loss repaid
  Of Corinth's sack, and Pydna's fatal day.

Imperial Rome! Though crime succeeded crime,
  As Earth fell prostrate neath her giant tread,
Still shall her subjects reap to endless time
  The priceless harvests by her wisdom spread.

What though the stern proconsul's iron rule
  Close followed on the legion's merciless sword?
Laws, arts, and culture, in that rigid school,
  Evoked a nation from each savage horde.

And when, at last, her crimes reacting wrought
  Their curse upon herself, to her, supine
And helpless, the Barbarian spoiler brought,
  With fire and sword, new life to her decline.

Theodoric, Clovis, Charles, your endless strife,
  From Weser's marsh to Naples' laughing bay,
Was but the throe that marked the nascent life,
  Emerging from the worn-out world's decay.

Ye were, amid that elemental war,
  But straws to show its course. Ye toiled, and won,

Or lost ; your people bled—yet slow and far
The mighty cause of man pressed ever on.

Long has the travail been. Kings, Kaisers, Popes,
   The rude Crusader and the Pagan Dane,
Each centred in his own ambitious hopes,
   But helped the cause he labored to restrain.

Hildebrand's voice sets Christendom on fire ;
   Neath Frederic's plough sinks Milan's lofty wall ;
Unnumbered victims glut De Montfort's ire ;
   From Ezzelin's dungeon shrieks the night appal—

If the tide ebbs, 'tis but to flow again.
   Each fierce convulsion gains some vantage ground.
Man's fettered limbs grow stronger, and the chain
   Falls link by link at each tumultuous bound.

The timid burgher dons the helm and shield,
   The wretched hind reluctant grasps the bow,
To fight their master's quarrels.   Courtrai's field
   And Sempach's hill that lesson's worth may show.

The restless soul still yearns for things unknown :
   It chafes against its fetters, seeks the way
That leads to freedom, but the sword alone
   Makes good the dreams that else would but betray.

See, Luther speaks, and Europe flies to arms:
   Her stubborn fight outlasts a hundred years,
A thousand fields her richest life-blood warms,
   Yet e'en the vanquished gain what pays their tears.

If Orange and Gustavus conquering died,
   Not Coligny nor Hampden fell in vain,
For one domain escaped the furious tide,
   And peace made that one desolate—faithful Spain!

So when men dallied with the treasonous theme—
   Equality for man on earth as heaven—
It was but speculation's idlest theme
   Till by the sword the time-wrought bonds were riven.

Though Moscow, Leipzig, Waterloo might seem
   To roll the tide back, they but marked its flood;
Nor could the Holy Allies' darkest scheme
   Restore the wrongs so well effaced in blood.

The end is not yet. God's mysterious way
   Evolves its purpose in its destined time.
Vainly we seek the fated march to stay—
   All things subserve it, wisdom, folly, crime.

We are His instruments.   The past has bled
For us.   We suffer for the future dim.
Then bravely face the darkness round us spread,
Do each his duty—leave the rest with Him !

INSCRIPTION FOR GETTYSBURG.   (1863.)

THE sternest valor in the holiest cause
    Exalted those whose hallowed dust lies here.
They fell for freedom, right, and equal laws,
    Nor vain the sacrifice, however dear.

Mourn not for them, but thank thy God that He
    Lifted their souls to meet their country's call.
Learn thou the duty that befits the free,
    And teach thy children thus to nobly fall !

www.ingramcontent.com/pod-product-compliance
Lightning Source LLC
Chambersburg PA
CBHW022339020726
47500CB00004B/1195